Green shoes, green socks and a bright green hat.

"Clive, you're a cabbage," his sister laughed.

een

Illustrated by
Leo Timmers

meadowside

Clive wore green.
Nothing else but green.

"You're a sprout,

you're a bean,

you're a little
green pea."

But Clive of course was none of these.

Clive wore green.
Green's what Clive liked.

Green jumpers, green shorts
and a bright green hat.

"Clive, you're an apple,"

his sister laughed.

"You're a leaf,

you're a lime,

you're a blade
of grass."

"I'm not," said Clive, "I'm something else."

Clive liked hats,
lots of hats.

Not blue or red,
but bright green hats.

"I'm a crocodile!" he cried.

And
he ate
her up.

For Alys P,
who liked Green the best
M.S

For my two big sisters,
Lia and Vera
L.T

First published in 2010
by Meadowside Children's Books
185 Fleet Street, London, EC4A 2HS

www.meadowsidebooks.com

Text © Mark Sperring 2010
Illustrations © Leo Timmers 2010

The rights of Mark Sperring
and Leo Timmers to be identified
as the author and illustrator of this work
have been asserted by them in accordance
with the Copyright, Designs
and Patents Act, 1988

A CIP catalogue record for this book
is available from the British Library

10 9 8 7 6 5 4 3 2 1

Printed in China